DIFFERENT!

Michael Buxton

Kane Miller
A DIVISION OF EDC PUBLISHING

Someone was hiding near the lagoon. It was a flamingo called Flo.

Flo never joined in.
She felt like she was
too different.

My beak is too big,
Flo thought.

"Beaks are amazing!"
said the other birds.

My neck is too long,
Flo thought.

"Long necks
are wonderful!"
said George.

My pink feathers are too bright, Flo thought.

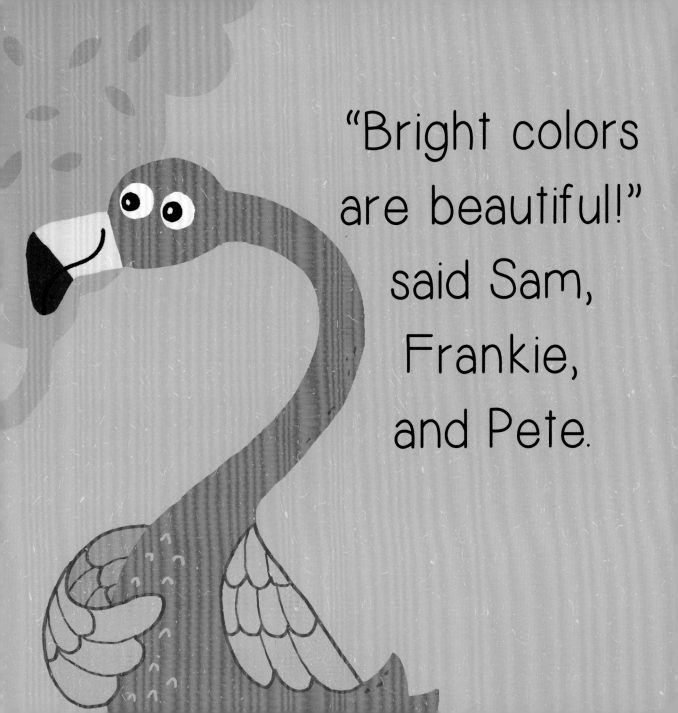

"Bright colors
are beautiful!"
said Sam,
Frankie,
and Pete.

My feet are too big,
Flo thought.

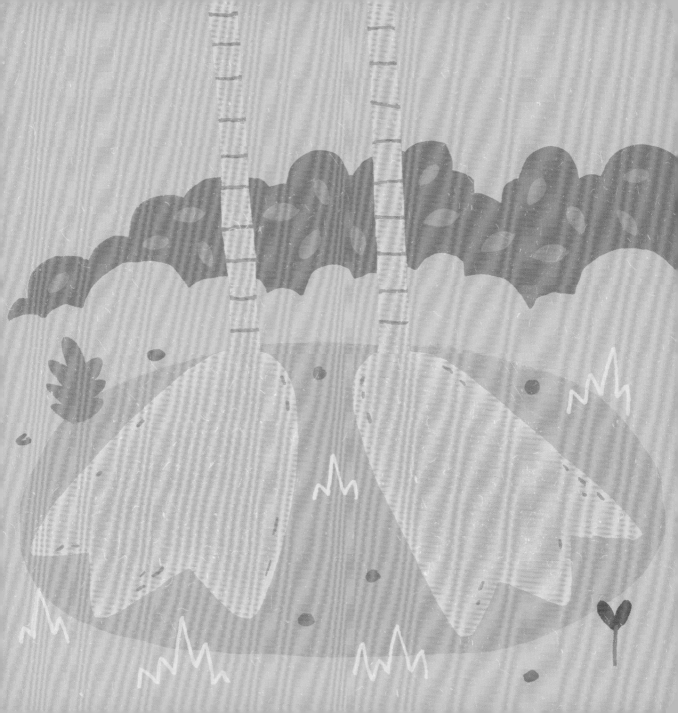

"Big, stompy feet are terrific!" said Ron.

Thanks to her friends,
Flo thought she was
very lucky to be ...